Puffin Books

THE GIZMO AGAIN

The girl sucks Jack's eye.
Her tongue is huge and spongy and dribbly.
The tip of it goes up one nostril.

Jack did something awful with an ice-cream –
now it's his turn to get licked.

A second gizmo yarn from
Australia's master of madness.

Other books by Paul Jennings

Unreal
Unbelievable
Quirky Tails
Uncanny
The Cabbage Patch Fib and *The Cabbage Patch War*
(both illustrated by Craig Smith)
The Paw Thing and *Singenpoo Strikes Again*
(both illustrated by Keith McEwan)
Unbearable
Round the Twist
Unmentionable
Undone
The Gizmo, Come Back Gizmo and
Sink the Gizmo
(all illustrated by Keith McEwan)
The Paul Jennings Superdiary
Uncovered
Wicked (with Morris Gleitzman)
Unseen
Uncollected

Picture Books

Grandad's Gifts
(illustrated by Peter Gouldthorpe)
Round the Twist
(graphic novel with Glenn Lumsden
and David de Vries)
The Fisherman and the Theefyspray
(illustrated by Jane Tanner)
Spooner or Later, Duck for Cover and
Freeze a Crowd
(all with Ted Greenwood and Terry Denton)

Paul Jennings

*Illustrated
by Keith McEwan*

PUFFIN BOOKS

Puffin Books
Penguin Books Australia Ltd,
487 Maroondah Highway, PO Box 257
Ringwood, Victoria 3134, Australia
Penguin Books Ltd,
Harmondsworth, Middlesex, England
Penguin Putnam Inc.
375 Hudson Street, New York, New York 10014, USA
Penguin Books Canada Limited,
10 Alcorn Avenue, Toronto, Ontario, Canada M4V 3B2
Penguin Books (N.Z.) Ltd,
Cnr Rosedale and Airborne Roads, Albany, Auckland, New Zealand
Penguin Books (South Africa) (Pty) Ltd
5 Watkins St, Denver Ext 4, 2094, South Africa
Penguin Books India (P) Ltd
11, Community Centre, Panchsheel Park
New Delhi 110 017, India

First published by Penguin Books Australia, 1995
10 9 8 7 6 5
Copyright © Greenleaves Pty Ltd, 1995
Illustrations Copyright © Keith McEwan, 1995

Typeset in Palatino by Midland Typesetters, Maryborough, Victoria
Made and printed in Australia by McPherson's Print Group

National Library of Australia
Cataloguing-in-Publication data:

Jennings, Paul, 1943–
The gizmo again.

ISBN 0 14 037807 3.

1. Short stories, Australian – 20th century. I. McEwan,
Keith II, Title.

A823.3

www.puffin.com.au

To Anthony

P.J.

1

Geeze, I'm looking forward to this.

My cake is so good that I feel weak at the knees. It's covered in strawberries and cream. All yummy and mushy.

I was going to eat a bit under the desk but Mr Billings saw me and gave me one of those looks that says 'Better not'. So I had to wait until lunch-time. My stomach has been rumbling all day. I have never been so hungry in all my life.

But now the big moment has arrived. I am sitting on a bench in the playground. All alone. I lick my lips. I open my mouth. I close my eyes to take the first bite. Oh, I am so hungry. This is going to be great. The smell is in my nostrils. My mouth is watering. There is nothing better than a scrumptious cake. Oh yes, yes, yes. I open my mouth wider.

Snatch.

What? What's this? It's gone. My lovely cake has gone before I can eat a crumb. Someone has grabbed it. Someone has stolen my dream cake.

Oh no. No, no, no. Not again. It is Gutsit and his gang. Already they are making off across the yard with my cake. I'll never get it back now. In any second it will be sliding down Gutsit's throat. They have done this before. Nearly every day they take the best bits of my lunch. And I just sit and put up with it.

No one but no one ever stands up to Gutsit. He is the

biggest kid in the school. Tough, mean and selfish. Nearby is the smallest kid – a new boy, Micky O'Shea.

He is also sitting all alone. The poor kid. He doesn't have any friends yet. You know what it's like in a new school.

'Hey,' I yell at Gutsit. 'You can't eat that. Give it back.'

Gutsit looks down at me. 'Can't I?' he says. 'Just watch me.'

I do watch him. With a sad heart and an empty stomach. I look on as he takes an enormous bite. I watch as half of my lovely lunch disappears down his cake-hole.

Gutsit and his two mates have been making my life miserable all year. They take my lunch.

They steal my pocket money. They twist my ears until they feel as if they are about to drop off.

Every day when I wake up I think about Gutsit's gang and worry about what they are going to do to me. It is the first thing I think about in the morning and the last thing I think about at night.

But now I have figured out a way to stop them. It is worth a try. I have been planning this for quite a while. It is the only way.

'Can I join the gang?' I say.

The three of them fall about laughing. 'What? A little runt like you?' says Ginger Gurk. 'What a joke.'

Gutsit holds up his hand. 'No, boys,' he says. 'We have to take this seriously. This young fellow wants to join. He could be tough – you never know. We have to give him a chance.'

I smile. This is good. If I join the gang they will not pick on me. They will leave me alone. 'Okay,' says Gutsit. 'You can join the gang. But you will have to be initiated.'

4

I am not sure what this means but I don't really care. Now that I am a member of the gang they will leave me alone and pick on someone else.

Gutsit takes another bite of my cake. What's left of it. 'Not bad,' he says. 'Not bad at all. Anyone like a bit?'

Micky O'Shea, the little new kid, is sitting nearby. He does not know what has been going on. When he hears Gutsit say, 'Anyone like a bit?' he nods his head. I nod my head too. I am so hungry.

Gutsit walks over to Micky O'Shea and gives him the rest of the cake. Straight in the face. He smashes my lovely cake all over Micky's face. The poor kid doesn't know what has happened. Gutsit and the other two think it is really funny. They cack themselves laughing at poor Micky O'Shea. He starts to wipe the cream off his cheeks. He even licks his lips and swallows a bit.

Micky does not complain. No one complains to Gutsit. He and his gang are the bosses of the whole school. They can do whatever they like. There is nothing anyone can do about it.

Not a single thing.

'Hey,' says Ginger Gurk. 'Look at this.'

Ginger Gurk is the second toughest member of the gang. He is looking at Micky's lunch-box. I have never seen a lunch-box like it before. It is made of hundreds of pieces of different types of wood. A picture of bread and carrots and food is carved into the lid. It sure is a beautiful box.

'My Grandad made it,' says Micky with a weak smile. 'He gave it to me just before he died.'

He presses a little brass switch and the lid springs open. Inside is the most delicious lunch you have ever seen. Mini pies, chocolates, half a mango all

ready to eat and a barbecued chicken leg. There is also a bottle of Coke.

Noblet, the third member of the gang, looks with greedy eyes. 'Ah ha,' he says with a leer that shows his yellow teeth. 'Just what I wanted.' He grabs the lunch-box before Micky can move. Noblet shoves a mini pie into his own mouth and swallows it in one go. Then he gives a loud burp and pats his stomach. The gang all laugh.

'Gross,' says Ginger Gurk.

Micky just stands there with cream all over his face looking like some sort of sad clown. He stares into the lunch-box as the gang start grabbing the food. 'Hey,' he says. 'My mum made that specially for – '

'Us,' yells Gutsit. 'Ain't that right, boys?'

'Yeah,' says Noblet as he wipes bits of mango off his lips. 'Didn't your mummy teach you to share?' He puts his mouth right up to Micky's nose and burps into his face. It is a horrible, loud burp all filled with mango and bad breath.

Poor Micky is nearly sick on the spot. The gang all fall about laughing.

I feel so sorry for Micky. He is all on his own. But I am secretly glad that the gang has forgotten about me. If I say anything they will start picking on me again. And anyway, I am a gang member now.

'Here,' Gutsit says to me. 'Eat this.' He hands me a chocolate. I don't really want to eat one of Micky's chocolates but now that I am a gang member I have to. I swallow the chocolate quickly without even tasting it. The gang gobble down the rest of Micky's lunch. There is nothing left. Except the Coke and the lunch-box.

Gutsit grabs the Coke and unscrews the lid. He puts his thumb over the end of the bottle. Then he shakes it up. Micky tries to run away but Ginger Gurk and Noblet grab his arms. Gutsit squirts the Coke all over Micky's face.

There is nothing he can do. He just stands there with his shoulders silently shaking. I know that inside he is crying a million tears. Even though we can't hear anything. All the food has gone. Soon this torture will all be over and Micky can go off and clean himself up. There isn't anything I can do. I am just not brave enough. And anyway, I belong to the gang.

'Can I have my lunch-box back, please?' Micky whispers.

'Sure you can have it back,' says Gutsit. He puts the lunch-box on the ground. We all look at it lying there. The little wood panels are twinkling in the sunlight.

'We'll just pack it up for you,' says Ginger Gurk.

Gutsit jumps high into the air and lands on the lunch-box with his big boots. He smashes the box into a zillion pieces.

Everyone in the school yard falls silent. It is the meanest thing ever. Gutsit, Ginger and Noblet walk off burping and shouting. Micky falls down onto his knees and starts to pick up the pieces. But it is hopeless. The box will never be a box again.

2

All afternoon I feel bad. Because of what happened to Micky. He was all alone and small. And he had no one to help him.

I also feel bad due to hunger pains. I have to go the whole day with nothing to eat. Every now and then my stomach gives a big rumble and everyone looks at me. Talk about embarrassing.

After school I hungrily make my way home. I feel bad about joining the gang but I had to. You know the old saying, 'If you can't beat them join them.' Well, that's what I've done. Now they will pick on someone else and leave me alone. Every time they do something mean to someone I will go to the loo or hide. That way I won't have to be mean myself. I will just look the other way.

Yes, joining the gang was the only way out.

At this very moment, would you believe, I see Gutsit and rest of our gang. There is a Mr Whippy van parked by the road. The gang are all stuffing their faces with double-dip chocolate and nuts.

My mouth starts to water. Soft ice-cream. I love it. I just love it. But I have no money. Maybe Gutsit will buy me one. He looks up as I approach. Then he pats me on the back. 'Here's our new member,' he says. Then he gives me his half-eaten double-dip chocolate-coated ice-cream.

My mouth starts to water. It is working already. He is being nice to me. Oh, I am so hungry. The ice-cream starts to melt down my fingers. I hold it up ready to lick. But a hand grabs my arm.

'Not so fast,' says Gutsit. 'It's not for you. It's for the next person who comes around the corner. If

you want to join the gang, you have to smash it in their face. That is your initiation test.'

Ginger Gurk and Noblet start to laugh and pat Gutsit on the back. My heart drops down into my boots. They are all jeering at me. They don't think I can do it. They think I am small and weak.

My face is burning. I am filled with shame. 'Okay,' I say. 'I'll do it.'

The gang all start to nod at each other. 'Impressive,' says Noblet. 'Very impressive.'

We all look at the corner. Waiting to see who will be the next person to come along. Ice-cream drips down onto the footpath. What a waste.

This is terrible. What have I done? What if a real big kid comes around the corner? He will flatten me for sure. Or Mr Billings. I couldn't smash an ice-cream in his face. Could I? I mean – he's a teacher. And anyway, I like him.

My own mother might be the next person round the corner. What have I done? 'Idiot, idiot, idiot,' I say to myself.

Footsteps. Someone is coming. Suddenly I am scared. Really frightened. My heart is pounding so loudly that I can hear it.

Then I see who it is. It is not Mr Billings. It is not a giant. It is not my mum. It is the last person in the world that I want it to be. It is Micky O'Shea. The poor kid, he has already suffered enough. Why did it have to be him?

As he comes nearer I hold the ice-cream ready. I feel terrible inside because he is a

lot smaller than me. But I have given my word. Everyone is watching. They will say I am a coward. They will not let me join the gang unless I do it. And anyway it's only ice-cream. It won't hurt much.

Micky reaches us. He is going by. 'Here,' I say. I smoosh the ice-cream straight in his face.

The poor little kid just looks at us. Just stands there and looks. He can't believe that it has happened twice in one day. His lips tremble under the melted ice-cream and chocolate.

Gutsit and the gang run off laughing. I go after them. 'Hey,' I say. 'Wait for me. I'm in the gang now.' They stop and look at me.

'Get real,' says Gutsit. 'You didn't really think we were going to let you join, did you? We wouldn't take a wimp like you.'

I just stand there. It can't be true. I try to stop myself from crying but the gang see my eyes watering. They laugh and jeer and then run off.

I walk slowly. I shouldn't have done it. Micky has gone so I can't even say sorry. Why was I so mean? I feel terrible. Guilty and hungry. That is how I feel.

The Mr Whippy van is still there. The owner is looking at me. He beckons me with his finger. What can he want? Maybe he has some old ice-cream to give away. He is a strange-looking man. He has weird eyes. You can see right through them. It looks as if it is raining inside his head.

'I saw what you did,' he says. 'Here, this is for you.' He puts something into my hand.

It is not an ice-cream. Nothing like it. It is some sort of metal gizmo. It is shaped like a ball with little coloured windows in it. When I look in the windows I can see that it is raining inside. It has a button saying ON. But no button saying OFF.

The little man clicks
the ON switch. Then he
just stands there smiling. It is
still raining inside his eyes. He
gives me the creeps so I turn and
run off. I don't even say thanks.

As I go I remember what my mother always says. 'Never take gifts from strangers.' I turn around to give the gizmo thing back. But it is too late. The Mr Whippy van is gone. It is just as if it was never there. The street is empty. That's funny, I didn't hear an engine start. This is weird.

I decide to toss the gizmo away. I don't want it. I don't want anything except maybe something to eat.

But it is not so easy to get rid of the gizmo.

It is stuck to my hand. It is joined to the skin of my palm and I can't let go.

No matter how hard I pull, it will not come away. It is just as if the gizmo is growing there in the palm of my hand. It is stuck to me. And I am stuck with it.

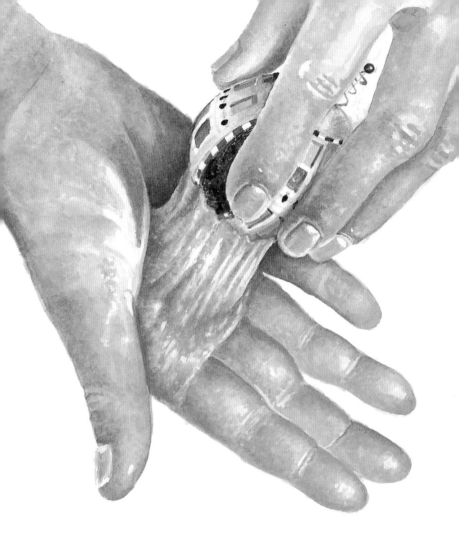

3

This is terrible. This gizmo thing has become a part of me. I pull as hard as I can. I try to peel it away. Ouch. It hurts like crazy. If I pull any harder it will rip the skin from my hand.

I'd better get home. I am going to need a doctor to cut the gizmo thing off. I walk slowly. I have to think about this. I can't tell Mum about pushing the ice-cream in Micky's face. No way. And she will give me a lecture about taking gifts from strangers. I have a big problem.

I take long, slow steps. As I go I notice something. Something strange. With every step a little light blinks on the gizmo. I stop and stand still. Nothing. No blinking red light. I take one step forward. The gizmo thing blinks red. What is going on here? This is crazy.

I try another step forward. Blink. And another. Blink. I look more closely. There is a little window with a number in it. Number eight. I take another step forward and the red light blinks again. Number nine. The gizmo is counting my steps. I have to get rid of this thing. I pull at it until tears of pain come into my eyes. It is no good. It just won't come off.

I take one more step. The gizmo blinks. And number ten appears. And then something else. It beeps. One loud beeping noise.

I feel funny. The world seems slightly different. I can't quite work out what it is but everything around me seems to have changed a bit. A cold feeling comes over me. I am scared. I have to admit it. I am scared. I start to run towards home. I am going to tell Mum everything. I don't like this at all.

With every step the gizmo blinks and adds one more number. When it gets up to twenty it suddenly beeps again.

I look around. What is it? Something's going on. The trees seem to have grown. I just can't figure it out. I slowly take another ten steps. Sure enough. Ten more blinks and then beep.

Aargh. The world is growing. The fences are bigger. The houses are bigger. I see someone coming with a skateboard under his arm. It is my old mate Spider Jeffries. He is so much bigger than me. The whole world and everyone in it has grown. I used to be taller than Spider.

He looks at me with a funny expression. 'Hey Jack,' he says. 'What's happened to you?'

'Everything's bigger,' I say. Is this a nightmare or what?

He shakes his head. He can't believe what he sees. His eyes grow wide and round. 'You've shrunk,' he says.

A feeling of terror rushes all over me. It is true. Oh no, it is true. The world is not bigger. I am smaller.

28

'It's this thing,' I shriek. 'This gizmo is shrinking me. Every time I take a step it makes me smaller. Look.'

I start to move forward and the counter clicks up more numbers. 'Beep.' It has reached forty. My arms actually shrink a little bit in front of my eyes. This is horrible. I have already shrunk to the size of one of the little kids in the bubs' class. If this goes on

I will be as small as a mouse by the time I reach home.

Why is this happening to me? Why? Why? Why?

I know. I shoved an ice-cream in Micky's face. I am a bully. I picked on a little kid. The strange man with the window eyes saw me. This gizmo thing is a punishment. And it is making me small and weak.

My mind goes into a panic. I try to think of some way of saving myself. I won't move. No way. With every ten steps the gizmo will make me smaller. 'Give me your skateboard,' I yell at Spider. 'Maybe if I don't walk I won't shrink.'

Spider just stands there looking down at me with his mouth hanging open. He isn't even listening to me so I just take the skateboard from his hands and push off. I snatch a glance at the gizmo as I speed along the footpath. It is not counting. It only works every time I take a step.

Phew. Things are not quite as bad as I thought. At least I will be able to get home without disappearing altogether. The footpath dips down and I start to pick up speed. Our house is just around the corner at the bottom of the hill. Nearly home. The skateboard goes faster and faster. It is too fast. It is going to overshoot the corner and plunge out onto the road. There are cars everywhere. I could be killed.

I bail out. I jump off that skateboard but my legs are pounding like crazy. It is all I can do to stop myself crashing to the ground. I run all the way to the bottom of the hill before I can stop.

Oh, the world is big. The people are giants. The houses are huge. Oh, oh, oh. I have shrunk right down. I am as small as a baby. I look up at Spider who has been running after me. I only come up to his knees. Spider's eyes grow wide. Then he starts to scream. His eyes bug out of his head. He turns and runs for it. He is so scared that he doesn't even take his skateboard with him.

I am alone on the footpath. No I'm not. Something is coming. Something huge and horrible.

4

A dog is loping along the street towards me. But to me it does not look like a dog. To me it is more like a horse. Shoot. It will probably think I'm a cat or something. I rush into a front garden and hide behind the letter-box. But this is a big mistake. I have run into the house where the dog lives. I know this dog. He's called Bluey. He has never liked me.

I crawl under some bushes and hide. By now I am as small as a rabbit. Bluey is snuffling around. He knows that something is in his territory. Dogs mark their territory by having a pee around the boundary. That is a warning to other dogs to keep out. Bluey will know if anyone has crossed his pee line.

Bluey stops. I peer up through the bushes. He is lifting up one of his back legs. Oh no. 'Please don't. Please Bluey. Nice Bluey. Don't, don't.' Bluey pees down through the bushes.

He covers me in it. I am showered in yellow dog pee. My clothes are dripping wet.

'No,' I scream. 'No, no, no.'

Oh, this is disgusting. It is terrible. This is the worst day of my life. I am soaked in wee. I am sopping wet.

Bluey hears me shouting. Squeaking would be more like it. Now that I am tiny my voice has changed to a squeal. Bluey sees me. He snuffles and pants. He puts his huge face right up to my little one. His breath is hot and wet and foul. Oh, yuck. I can't take much more of this.

But there is worse to come. Bluey growls. Then he grabs me by the back of my t-shirt and picks me up. He trots out of the garden and down the road. 'Stop,' I yell. 'Stop, stop, stop.' But Bluey does not stop. He jogs down the middle of the road. Up down, up down. He is shaking me about like a loose bag of bones. My brain is rattling around inside my skull.

Bluey's horrible wet tongue is hanging out of his mouth. Dribble is running down all over me and mixing with the pee.

I close my eyes and grit my teeth as Bluey runs along the street with me dangling out of his mouth. It can't get any worse than this. It just can't.

Yes it can.

A pack of dogs come around the corner. They see me. They want me. They probably think I am something good to eat. Quick as lightning Bluey bolts into a shopping arcade. Faster and faster he goes. The pack follow, barking and howling. I am swinging around like an old bit of meat in Bluey's mouth.

Suddenly Bluey stops. He turns and starts snarling at the other dogs. The sound is terrible. As loud as a jet engine, growling and rumbling next to my ears. Bluey suddenly tosses his head back and lets go. He gives a bark. To my little ears it is like a volcano erupting. But I can't worry about that because I am spinning and turning high in the air. It is a long way down. A few metres seems high when you are only the size of a rabbit.

Whump. I hit the footpath. The wind is knocked from my lungs. I can't breathe and I can't move.

The dogs snarl and snap and bite each other.

They stand on me. 'Ouch, ooh.' It hurts. Oh, I am scared. I try to roll away but I can't move.

A hand reaches down and grabs me. I am saved.

'Look, Mummy,' says a voice.

It is a little girl. Well, once I would have thought she was a little girl. But now I think she is a giant. She waves me around like –

'A doll,' she says. 'It's mine, it's mine, it's mine.'

I try to breathe. I try to say, 'I'm not a doll.' But nothing comes out. I just can't snatch a breath.

Another giant face bends down. It is her mother. She stares into my face. 'It is too,' she says. 'It's one of those Baby Alive dolls. But isn't it ugly?'

Ugly? Who's ugly? I'm not ugly.

'It's got a ball in its hand,' says the giant girl. She starts to pull at the gizmo but it won't budge. Oh, the pain. She nearly yanks my hand off.

'It's so real,' says a man's voice. Her father bends down and peers at me. 'They even make them wet their pants now, you know. Imitation wee. You can smell it. It must have cost a bomb. We'll have to hand it in.'

The girl does not like this one bit. 'I want it, I want it, I want it,' she screams.

She is shaking me around so hard that my head feels as if it is about to fall off.

'Let her keep it for now,' says the mother. 'We can hand it in later and buy her another one.'

'No,' says the brat. 'I love this one. I just love it.'

Without warning she puts her face next to mine. For a moment I am not sure what is going on. There is something wet and soft on my face. No, no, no. She is licking my face. Next she sucks my eye. So hard that it feels as if my eyeball is going to plop out. Then she sucks my nose. Her tongue is huge and spongy and dribbly. The tip of it goes up one nostril. She is putting her tongue up my nose.

Oh, foul, foul, foul. Help me. Please, someone help me. The brat is sucking my face with her giant mouth. I can't breathe. I can't talk. I can't stand it.

Everything goes black.

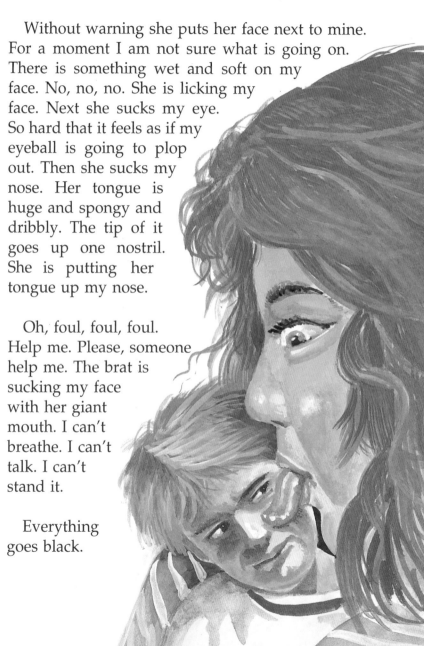

5

The next thing I know I am lying on something soft. I don't open my eyes at first. I hope it is all a bad dream. I hope that I will open my eyes and find myself in my bedroom. Full size.

I don't have to open my eyes. A giant finger does it for me. It is the girl. A huge, dirty fingernail lifts up my eyelid. 'Look,' she says. 'It can open its eyes.'

The giant brat grabs me and shoves me into a toy high-chair. I see that she has a toy tea-set. Toy plastic knives and forks and plates. They are all set out for a tea party.

'Help me,' I shout. 'Please help.' I try to climb out but the girl pushes me down and straps me in.

'Be a good boy,' says brat face.

'I am not a doll,' I squeak. 'I am a human being.'

'Incredible,' says the mother. 'It talks too.'

She peers even more closely. 'John,' she yells. 'Come and look at this.' She rushes out of the room to get her husband.

This can't get any worse. It just can't.

Yes it can.

The girl starts to mix up something on one of the plates. She puts in flour and salt and pepper and mustard. Then she spits into the mixture about six times and stirs it all up. It is a horrible, spitty, smelly mess. She puts some on the end of a spoon. Then she looks at me.

41

'Open up,' she says. Oh no. She is going to feed me. I grit my teeth but it is no good. I am too small. She pushes the mixture into my mouth and holds my jaw closed with her fingers.

The taste is terrible. I want to vomit but I can't because my mouth is held closed.

'Naughty boy. Eat your din dins,' she says.

I am choking. There is only one thing to do. I swallow the revolting mix.

'Good boy,' says the horrible little girl. She starts putting more on the spoon.

'Stop,' I yell. 'Stop, stop, stop.'

She is coming. With the spoon. I undo the straps and jump up to the window-sill. It is a long way down to the ground outside but I don't worry about it. Out I go. Down, down, down.

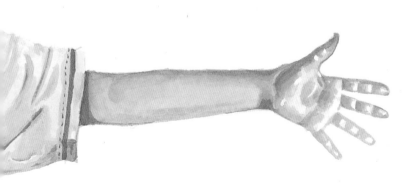

Crash, I land in some bushes. I can't believe this –
I have been sucked, licked and shaken. I am
scratched and sore. Is there no end to it?

No there isn't. I hear a voice coming from the
window. 'My doll ran away,'
it screams.

'Nonsense,' says the man's
voice. 'It's not that good.'

The voices come closer so I run for it.
The gizmo beeps as I go. Oh no, not
that. If I run I will shrink. But if I
stop it's back to the high-chair.
Anything is better than the
high-chair. I keep running. I am
shrinking. By now I am the
size of –

'A rat,' says the man's
voice. 'There's a rat in the
garden. Quick. Get the cat.'

There is a small forest
on the edge of the
garden. If I can reach
it I will be safe.
There is a lot of
yelling and shouting.

I look behind me. A cat comes leaping out of the window. It is after me. Run, run, run. Go, man, go. Or you are dead.

I reach the edge of the forest at the same time as the cat. By now I am the size of a mouse. The cat is enormous. It swipes me with a paw and sends me flying. It is toying with me. It wants me to run. It is going to play with me before it eats me.

The cat is not a cat. Not to me. It is a tiger the size of an elephant. Its teeth are terrible spears. Its whiskers are wire rope. Its breath is a storm from hell.

And I am a boy made of jelly. I shiver and wobble before the dreadful beast. This is the end. I am gone. 'Oh, heaven help me. Please don't let it munch my bones. Please make it go away.'

The cat crouches. 'Don't jump. Please, please, please.' I look around. There is nowhere for me to go.

Except backwards.

Slowly, slowly. Don't annoy it. Back, back, back. Gently now. I keep walking backwards. The cat quivers but it doesn't move. It knows it can get me whenever it wants. Its tail is like a giant snake waiting to strike.

I keep stepping backwards. I take about ten paces. The gizmo beeps.

I feel funny. The world seems slightly different. I can't quite work out what it is but everything around me seems to have changed a bit. A cold feeling comes over me. I don't like this at all.

I look at the gizmo. With every step backwards it blinks and subtracts a number. I take about ten more steps and it beeps again.

I look around. What is it? Something's going on. Everything is different. The trees seem to have shrunk. I just can't figure it out. I quickly take another ten steps backwards. Sure enough. Ten more blinks and then – beep.

Ah. Yes. I am growing. The trees are shrinking. The bushes are shrinking. The whole world and everything in it is getting back to normal.

A feeling of hope rushes all over me. It is true. Oh yes, it is true. I am taller.

The gizmo is enlarging me. Every time I take a step backwards it makes me bigger.

The cat is still creeping forward and licking its lips. I keep moving backwards and the counter subtracts more numbers. 'Beep.' My hands actually grow a little bit in front of my eyes. This is wonderful. I have already grown to the size of one of the little kids in the bubs' class. If this goes on I will be back to normal in no time.

The cat can't believe what has happened. It looks up at me. It has never seen someone grow so quickly. Its hair stands on end. The poor thing gives a yowl and scampers up a tree.

I smile and keep going. With every step I take backwards, one number is subtracted. Soon it is back to zero. And I am back to my old self. Not one bit bigger or smaller.

Just then the girl and her parents rush into the garden. They look straight at me. All they see is an ordinary boy. 'Have you got my doll?' says the little brat. She does not recognise me now that I am back to my normal size.

I just shake my head and they move off into the bushes. They are looking for a doll and a rat. But they won't find either.

I head for home as fast as I can go.

6

The gizmo is still stuck to my hand. It still beeps every ten steps. And still makes me smaller when I walk forwards.

But I use my brains. I walk ten steps backwards and ten steps forwards. When I walk forwards I shrink and when I step backwards I grow. In the end I arrive home without attracting attention.

I run into my room and think about my problem. I am my normal size. That is good. That is great. That is fantastic. But I can't keep growing and shrinking like this. I know what I have to do. I have to go around and see Micky O'Shea. It is dangerous but I must make up for being a bully.

The trip takes quite a while. Ten steps forwards and ten back. Up, down. Up, down. In the end I arrive at Micky's place. I am exactly the right size. I stand at the front gate. I don't want to move until this is over. 'Hey, Micky,' I yell. 'I need to talk to you.'

Micky's face appears at the window. He looks out and sees the kid who smashed the ice-cream into his face – me. He does not want to come out and I don't blame him.

'It's not a trick,' I shout. 'Please come out.'

After a bit Micky appears at the door. He walks slowly down the path. He doesn't trust me. He probably thinks the gang are going to jump out and grab him.

When he reaches the gate I hang my head. 'I'm sorry about the ice-cream,' I say. 'It was a mean thing to do. I wanted to join the gang to stop them stealing my lunch every day.'

I hold out my hand. 'Shake?' I say.

Micky doesn't move. He just looks at me. Then he holds out his hand.

As he does so, something wonderful happens. The gizmo comes unstuck. It just drops to the ground.

We shake hands and smile.

'How about an ice-cream?' says Micky. 'I've got two dollars.'

An ice-cream. Suddenly I realise. I haven't had anything to eat all day except for one chocolate and a mouthful of spit and mush. 'Let's go,' I say.

I pick up the gizmo and put it in my pocket. It doesn't blink. It doesn't beep. It doesn't do anything. I know that I am safe from it now.

Micky and I wander down to the milk bar and he buys us an ice-cream each. We take them outside and stand on the footpath.

Geeze, I'm looking forward to this.

I've had almost nothing to eat all day. I am famished. I have never been so hungry in all my life.

But never mind. Lucky for me Micky had some money. Two dollars. And he

has bought me an ice-cream. It is the most glorious one in the whole world. Creamy, with strawberries all mushy and yummy.

The big moment has arrived. After everything that has happened to me. I lick my lips. I open my mouth. I close my eyes to take the first bite. Oh, I am so hungry. This is going to be great. The smell is in my nostrils. My mouth is watering. There is nothing better than a scrumptious ice-cream. Oh yes, yes, yes. I open my mouth wider.

Snatch.

What? What's this? It's gone. My lovely ice-cream has gone before I can take a lick. Someone has grabbed it. Someone has stolen my ice-cream.

Oh no. No, no, no. Not again. It is Gutsit and his gang. I'll never get it back now. In any second it will be sliding down Gutsit's throat. He has my ice-cream. And Micky's. The gang have done this before.

I race after them. I can't believe what I am doing. No one but no one ever stands up to Gutsit. He is the biggest kid in the school.

Gutsit and the gang stare at me. There are three of them. And only two of us. They will wipe the floor with us. They are big and tough and mean.

I am shaking at the knees. But I find courage from somewhere. I snatch my ice-cream from Gutsit's hand. 'I'll take that,' I say.

Gutsit's eyes nearly pop out. He is mad. He is furious. He can't believe that someone like me is standing up to him. The gang close in. They are the toughest kids in the school.

Micky stands next to me. He is going to back me up even though we don't have a chance.

There is no way we can beat them.

Suddenly there is a beep from my pocket. It is the gizmo. It is trying to tell me something.

I take it out of my pocket and immediately it sticks to my hand. But I am not worried. Well not much anyway.

The gang close in. I start to back away. They come after me. They see me going backwards. 'The little wimp's scared stiff,' sneers Gutsit.

After ten steps the gizmo beeps and I grow a bit bigger. I walk backwards faster. The gang come after me.

'Beep, beep, beep.'

The gang stop. I keep going. Their mouths fall open. They look up at me. With every step backwards I grow taller. I am as big as a horse. I am as big as a house.

I am so big that I can see into the next street.

The gang scream and start to run. I could step on them and squash them if I wanted. But I don't. Instead I pick them up and hold them in my hands.

I hold them up close to my face. Very close. I can hear them yelling and squealing. They don't know what I am going to do.

They don't have to worry. I am not going to hurt them. After all, I'm not a bully. Am I?

Just then my stomach gives a rumble. It is so long since I have eaten that it just won't be quiet. I try to hold back but I can't. I open my mouth and let out a burp. It is like a thousand thunderstorms put together. It is the loudest, smelliest burp in the history of the world. It just about blows their heads off.

They are yelling and screaming. They are scared out of their wits. 'Don't worry, boys,' I boom out. 'I won't hurt you.'

I put them gently on the ground and they start to run. Ginger Gurk goes one way and Noblet goes the other. Gutsit seems to be winded and doesn't move for a bit.

I put the giant ice-cream down and start to walk forwards. 'Beep, beep, beep.' Soon I am back to my normal size.

I look at the gizmo. It unsticks itself and bounces over to Gutsit. Before he can blink it is fixed to the palm of his hand. Gutsit gives a terrible scream and starts to run. As he goes he grows smaller and smaller. Soon he is about the size of a doll.

At that very moment who should come round the corner but the little brat and her mother. She sees Gutsit. 'My doll,' she screams.

Her mother looks at Gutsit. 'It's even uglier than before,' she says.

The little girl picks up Gutsit and shakes him about. She thinks he is her doll. 'Naughty boy,' she says. Then she does something terrible. Awful. I try not to smile when I see what she does to Gutsit.

She looks down the back of his pants. 'Naughty boy,' she says. 'You've done a poo.' Quick as a flash she pulls down Gutsit's pants. Then she grabs his ankles in one hand and lifts up his legs. She takes out a handkerchief and starts to wipe his bottom. Gutsit yells and screams and howls as the little girl wipes away like crazy. It must be quite a while since he has had his bottom wiped and he does not like it one little bit.

Finally the little girl stops wiping. 'Come on,' she says to Gutsit. 'It's dinner-time. Time to go home.'

And it is time for me to go too. Gutsit is going to get a dose of the high-chair. It couldn't happen to a nicer person.

Just as I turn to leave I notice a Mr Whippy van. And a funny little man with eyes like windows. It seems to be raining inside his head. He is looking at Gutsit and chuckling.

Micky stares at me with big round eyes. His knees are knocking and his mouth is hanging open. He can't believe what he has just seen. I can hardly believe it myself.

'Don't worry,' I say. 'Everything is okay. No one is going to pick on us after this.'

I point to the giant ice-cream which is still where I put it. Micky and I stand there and lick our lips. We have never seen an ice-cream as big as a car before.

'Come on,' I say to Micky. 'Let's get stuck into it before it melts.'